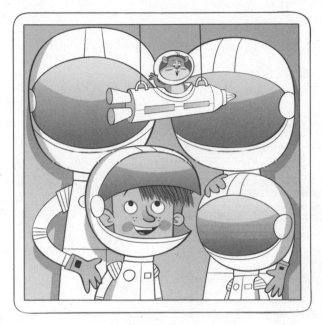

THE JINKS FAMILY
Me, Lucy, Mum Dad and Stinky

To my mum and dad, who took me to the library.

Chapter 1

I rushed home from school, burst into my bedroom and told my hamster the news.

'I'm going to make a rocket!' I announced.

I was expecting him to be excited, or at least a tiny bit *interested*.

I should have known better.

'Make a rocket?' he spluttered. 'You'd struggle to make a *sandwich*.' He'd been having a nap, and he was always a bit cranky when he'd just woken up. 'You probably can't *spell* "rocket",' he added, 'let alone make one.'

'That's why I need your help, Stinky.'

He squinted at me through the bars of his cage. 'And why on earth do you want to build a rocket?' he asked.

I pulled a piece of paper from my pocket, unfolded it and showed it to him.

'Just imagine it though, Stinky – our very own space rocket. *Whoosh!*'

'*Whoosh?* Do you even have the faintest idea how to build a rocket?'

'Do you?'

'I most certainly do,' he said.

'And so if I get all the stuff we need, will you build it with me?'

'Of course not,' he said.

I groaned. Sometimes it was brilliant having a furry little genius living with me. But sometimes I wished I had a goldfish instead, or a budgie, or at least a hamster without an attitude problem.

'I look after you really well,' I said. 'I give you fresh salad every day and clean out your poo twice a week, but when I ask you for just a *tiny* bit of help–'

'In case you hadn't noticed,' he interrupted, 'I'm a hamster.'

'I had noticed actually.'

'These paws of mine –' he poked one through the bars of his cage for me to inspect – 'are approximately one centimetre long.'

'And?'

'So how do you think I'll be able to use scissors? Or glue? Or mix rocket fuel? Or perform any part of the rocket-building process whatsoever?'

I scratched my head.

'I hadn't really thought about any of that,' I admitted glumly. 'That's it then, I suppose – no rocket.'

'Unless you make it,' he suggested.

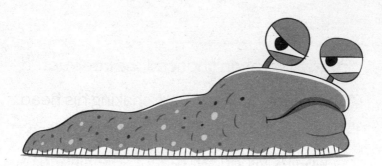

'But I could never do it on my own. I'm not clever like you.'

'Well, that's perfectly true, Ben. You have the intelligence of a slug. And not a high-achieving slug either. But what if I were to give you step-by-step instructions? Instructions that even *you* could understand?'

I clapped my hands together excitedly. 'So what do we need?'

'For the main body of the rocket,' he started, 'we need something that is both strong and cylindrical.'

'*Cylindri-what?*'

'Good grief,' he muttered, shaking his head. 'The boy wants to build a rocket but he doesn't know what "cylindrical" means.' He sighed. 'A tube or a pipe, for instance, is *"cylindrical"*. Something long and round – that shape is a *cylinder*. Don't they teach you anything at school?'

'Not really,' I said.

'What did you learn today, for example?'

'Nothing much. Oh, wait – Stuey Jones taught me how to burp the alphabet.'

Stinky sighed – a very loud sigh for such a small rodent. But before I could even get to 'D' in my burping demonstration, I was interrupted by a very loud noise indeed.

My mum.

She usually had a normal voice, like a regular person, but when it was teatime (or when she was angry – which was quite often these days) she had this huge shriek like an opera singer who'd just dropped a heavy brick onto her big toe.

'*Ben!*' she yelled from the kitchen (though she could have been in another town and I'd still have heard her), '*tea's ready!*'

Stinky wished me luck. He knew what my family was like.

**Ben!
Tea's ready!**

Chapter 2

It was beans on toast for tea. Again.

It was always something on toast these days. In the last week my mum had made:

- **Beans on toast** (three times)
- **Egg on toast** (twice)
- **Alphabetti Spaghetti on toast** (only once, because my sister stormed off after I'd spelt out a message on my plate. Mum went bananas at me. Dad corrected my spelling).

Then, just when you thought teatime couldn't

possibly get any worse, yesterday we actually had:

- **Toast on toast** (though Mum pointed out that there was a bit of cheese in the middle and so it was technically a toasted cheese sandwich).

The four of us – me, Mum, Dad and my little sister, Lucy – were sitting round the kitchen table, when Lucy screwed up her face.

'I *hate* beans,' she whined. 'And I hate toast. And I really, really hate beans on toast.'

'Don't use the "H" word,' my mum said, frowning. 'Just say they're *not your favourite*.'

'Beans are really, really, really, really not my favourite,' Lucy said, grimacing.

'Cheer up, Lucy,' said Dad, deciding it was time for *his* favourite – and only – poem:

'Beans, beans, good for your heart, The more you eat, the more you f—'

'*Derek!*' my mum interrupted. 'Not at the table, thank you.'

'Stuff on toast all the time is pretty boring,

Mum,' I said. I didn't usually agree with Lucy about anything, but this time she had a point.

My mum took a deep breath. 'The truth is,' she said, 'money is a little bit tight these days.'

'Tight?' Lucy said.

'It means we're broke,' I explained. 'We're skint. We've got no money.'

'It means,' my mum told my sister, ignoring me, 'that we just have to be a tiny bit more *careful*, that's all.'

Then she glared at Dad, which made me think he'd been betting on horses again.

'Couldn't Ben get a job?' asked Lucy, who was always making helpful suggestions like this.

'He's only nine,' Mum explained. 'There are actual laws against him working. Though it *would* be nice if he spent a bit less time in his bedroom.'

'Sometimes I hear him talking to his hamster,' Lucy said, giggling.

I needed to change the subject fast.

'We could always sell Lucy's Barbies,' I suggested. 'You know – to raise a bit of money.'

'Hey!' said my sister, kicking me under the table. 'Not fair.'

'We won't be selling anything,' Mum said firmly. 'But the truth is, we won't be buying much either. So that means we can't get you much for your birthday, Ben.' I groaned. My sister sniggered. 'And I'm sorry, Lucy,' Mum continued, 'but we also can't buy those new tap shoes you wanted.'

Lucy's smirk became an angry pout.

'*But, Mum!*' she screeched. '*You absolutely promised! Everyone else has a new pair!*'

She scraped back her chair, stood up and stomped off to her room. Her tap-dance training had made her a world-class stomper. The house seemed to shake with every step. My mum followed her, sighing.

'I hate this family!' yelled Lucy.

My dad shook his head. 'I think she meant to say that this family isn't her favourite,' he muttered, before shovelling another forkful of beans into his mouth.

It was the beans that gave me the great idea.

'Cans are cylindrical, right, Dad? Cans of beans?'

He nodded, then grinned. '*Cylindrical* – that's a big word for you, Ben. They teach you that at school, did they?'

I nodded. Well, I could hardly tell him I learned it from my hamster, could I? He'd think I'd gone completely nuts.

'Can I take two empty beans cans to my room, Dad?'

'Sure,' he said, then squinted at me suspiciously. 'You're not *up* to something, are you?' he asked, with a smile.

I shook my head. 'Just a bit of homework,' I said.

And it was true, in a way.

Chapter 3

Miss Miles was my new teacher and unlike my old teacher, Mr McCreedy, she was great, and not at all evil. Right now she was looking around the classroom.

'So,' she said, 'who has decided to make something for this year's science competition then?'

Edward Eggington put his hand up, as usual.

He was probably *born* with his hand up.

Edward Eggington was:

a) a know-it-all

b) a bully

c) better than me at pretty much everything,

and, worst of all,

d) my next-door neighbour.

'Only Edward?' she said, looking a bit disappointed.

'It's not worth entering, miss,' Lisa Chan explained. 'Edward wins every year.'

'Or his *dad* does,' said Stuey Jones.

Everyone laughed. Well, everyone except Edward Eggington, who scowled at Stuey and whispered, 'At least my dad's not a chimpanzee.'

STUEY JONES'S DAD

CHIMPANZEE

It wasn't a nice thing to say at all. Stuey Jones's dad wasn't a chimpanzee, though he was small and very hairy.

Edward Eggington's dad, however, was a proper scientist, and we all knew that it was *him* who made last year's winning entry. The theme was Weather, and most kids made a little pot that measured how much it had rained, or one of those paper windmills that whizz around in the breeze. The Eggingtons, though, built this incredible solar-powered Snow Machine. The sunnier the weather, the more snow it made. In the middle of summer, people were actually playing snowballs on the school field.

When he won, Edward was on the front page of the newspaper, next to the Snow Machine, holding the prize-money cheque and wearing a stupid big grin on his face.

Edward Eggington just loved being the centre of attention.

I'm not like that. I'm not a putting-my-hand-up kind of person at all. It's my *hamster* who knows everything. Not me. I don't really like to be noticed.

But here I was now, *with my hand actually in the air.*

'Yes, Ben?' said Miss Miles, probably thinking that I needed the toilet.

'I've been working on something for the competition too.'

She beamed. 'Great! Working on what?'

'A rocket.'

'A model?'

'No. One that goes *whoosh* up into the sky.'

There were some giggles, which Miss Miles ignored. 'And what are you making it out of, Ben?'

'Two old baked-bean cans.'

The whole class now erupted into laughter. Edward Eggington in particular was laughing so hard I expected to see snot coming out of his nose any second. It took a long time for everyone to calm down. 'Well,' Miss Miles said. 'I can't wait to see your launch. Now, Edward, what's *your* idea?'

Edward neatly folded a tissue and dabbed the tears of laughter from his eyes.

A-HA-HA
HA-HA-HA-HA
HA-HA
HA-
HA!!

'A flying saucer,' he announced. 'Better than any drone you can buy. And it will be like nothing that the world has ever seen.'

There was silence in the class, apart from a few gasps of astonishment.

Suddenly my baked-bean-can rocket didn't sound very good at all.

Unless...

It was then that I had another brilliant idea.

I'd need Stinky's help again, of course. I could hardly wait for school to finish so I could run home and ask him.

Chapter 4

'**N**o way,' said Stinky. 'Absolutely not.'

'Oh, come on,' I said. 'Think about it at least.'

'If you think I'm going to sit inside *that* thing –' he jabbed a tiny paw towards the rocket – 'as it's hurtling into the sky at ninety-six kilometres per hour, you must be completely crackers.'

'You're not afraid of heights, are you, Stinky?'

'Are you out of your mind? Of *course* I'm

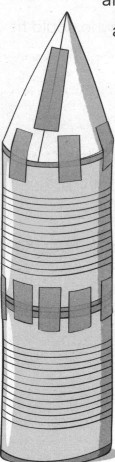

afraid of heights. All hamsters are afraid of heights. That's what happens when you're seven centimetres tall.'

I looked at the rocket on my desk next to Stinky's cage, and sighed. It wasn't finished yet – just two shiny cans superglued together and a pointy cardboard nose-cone fixed on top.

'Edward Eggington next door is building some kind of incredible flying saucer,' I told him, 'and ours is just two old tins going up in the air and coming back down again. But if there was something – or *someone* – who could fit inside and control it – doing a loop-the-loop, for example, or writing a word in the sky – *then* we'd be in with a chance.'

He shrugged.

'It's not fair,' I complained. 'Edward Eggington's getting help from his dad.'

'And you're getting help from *me*,' said Stinky.

'That's different. Animals don't count.'

'Oh, thanks,' he snapped.

'I didn't mean it like that. It's just that his dad's an actual scientist. So,' I said, 'don't you want to be the first hamster in space?'

'Not a bit.'

'But you could go up to the Moon, Stinky,

and get some cheese. Imagine *that*!'

He stared at me and was actually speechless for a while.

A very short while.

'First of all,' he said wearily, 'let me remind you – hamsters don't like cheese. It gives us stomach ache. Secondly, the Moon is made out of rock and dust. Not cheese. Thirdly, a rocket the size of two baked-bean cans will not get anywhere near the Moon.'

'It'll be *fun* though,' I said. 'Imagine the feeling of wind in your fur.'

'No, thank you.'

'Scaredy-cat.'

'Actually,' he said, 'cats are relatively brave animals. *Rabbits*, on the other hand, are a

bunch of absolute chickens. And chickens, well – they're the biggest chickens of all.'

'So says the hamster who's scared of flying.'

'It's not the *flying* that I'm afraid of. It's the *crashing* part, and the *exploding into smithereens* part that frighten the life out of me.'

'But you designed the rocket,' I reminded him. 'And you're a genius.'

'That's true,' he said. 'But what goes up must come down. More particularly, what goes *zooming* up into the sky must come *crashing* down. And I have no intention of being inside it when it does.'

I groaned. But I had one more tactic to try.

'If we win,' I told him, 'I'll be able to buy you all the carrots you can eat.'

His little eyes lit up.

'Really?' he said. He'd been having to eat grain a lot recently, because of our money troubles.

He went for a run on his wheel and, when he hopped off, he faced me.

'OK', he said, wheezing. 'It's a deal. But we have to make the rocket safe first.'

'Of course,' I said. 'How?'

'I have an idea,' he said. 'But we'll need your mum's help.'

Chapter 5

Guess what was for tea that night?

I'll give you a clue: it begins with 'B' and ends with 'eans-on-toast'.

The four of us were in our usual positions around the kitchen table. Lucy was grumbling, my dad was stuffing his face and my mum was talking about the weather, which was her favourite subject these days. It *had* been raining a lot around here recently.

But then I said something that made everyone stop and stare at me.

'Mum,' I said, 'could you teach me how to sew, please?'

My dad almost choked on his toast. My mum's eyebrows shot up in surprise. And Lucy snorted with laughter.

'Sewing?' she said, giggling. 'That's for *girls*.'

'It most certainly is not,' my mum said. 'Was Valentino a girl? Was Versace a girl?'

'Maybe,' I said, shrugging. 'I've never heard of them.'

'They're famous fashion designers,' my dad explained, looking very pleased with himself for knowing this.

My mum nodded at him approvingly. 'I would *love* to teach you to sew, Ben,' she said enthusiastically. 'What a nice idea. We can start tonight. We'll make a pencil case. That was the first thing I learned to sew with *my* mum.'

'I was actually thinking more about making a *parachute*, Mum.'

Now it was my dad's turn to laugh.

'A *parachute*?' he said. 'A parachute? You thinking of jumping out of an aeroplane, are you, son?'

'It's not for me,' I said. 'It's for . . .' And then I didn't actually know what to say. It was probably best that they didn't know about the rocket yet. They might think it was dangerous. And it was certainly best they didn't know that my hamster would be inside it. 'It's for my Action Man,' I said eventually. I had an old one in my bottom drawer.

Lucy giggled. 'He wants to make a parachute for one of his dolls!'

'An Action Man is *not* a doll,' I said. 'It's an action figure. There's a difference. A big difference.'

'Anyway,' my mum said to all of us, 'I think it's great that Ben's interested in learning such a useful thing. A parachute might be an *unusual* first thing to make, but I'd be very happy to teach you, Ben.'

I grinned.

After tea I raced back to my room to work some more on the rocket and tell my hamster the good news.

Chapter 6

I was in my room when I had a sudden feeling that someone was watching me, and not just Stinky either. He *had* to watch me, he said, to make sure that the rocket was 100% safe.

No, I felt like someone *else* was watching me. I glanced at my bedroom door, but it was closed. No Lucy. No Mum or Dad.

It was Stinky who saw it first.

'Look!' he said, jabbing a paw towards the window.

There, hovering just outside, was a small

flying saucer, like a silver frisbee.

'Aliens!' I gasped, leaping out of my chair.

'Don't be so ridiculous,' said Stinky. 'It's Edward Eggington of course. If you look down into his garden, you'll probably see him operating the control.'

Sure enough, there he was, grinning up at me, waving with one hand, while the other one controlled the flying saucer. Then he stuck his tongue out at me and made a face.

I opened the window to yell something down at him, but I suddenly couldn't think of anything to say. *He* could though:

'Hey, Beany Boy!' he called. 'I thought you might want to see what a *real* science project looks like.'

The flying saucer *did* look pretty amazing, I had to admit. It was a silver plastic disc and it hovered just out of reach.

I shook my head at Edward Eggington and shut the window. But before I could close the curtains, Stinky said:

'Let me have a closer look at that thing.'

So I scooped him out of his cage.

'Careful!' he snapped. 'Have you any idea how frightening it is, being carried around by someone so clumsy?'

I cupped my hands and held him next to the window.

'What are those little pipes sticking out of it?' I asked him. 'Are they *lasers* or something?'

Stinky shook his head. There were six little bumps on top of the disk, and each bump had a tiny pipe poking out of it.

'I don't know,' he said. 'But I do get the feeling that he's up to something. Something bad. And I would rather like to find out what.'

We stared at the flying saucer as it zoomed back to Edward Eggington like a bird returning to its owner.

When I pulled the curtains shut, I heard a squeak, and it wasn't Stinky. He wasn't the squeaky type. It was the squeak of a *door*. My bedroom door. I spun around to see Lucy poking her head in.

'What are you doing?' she asked, frowning.

'Nothing,' I said. 'Buzz off.'

She was staring at the
rocket on the desk.

'What's that?' she said.

'Homework.'

She scrunched
up her forehead
into an even
bigger frown.

'Who were you
just talking to?'
she asked.

'Nobody.'

'I heard you – were you
talking to your hamster
again?'

'No.'

'It sounded as if *he* was talking too. Was he talking?'

'No. Hamsters don't talk, Lucy.'

'So you were putting on a funny voice to make it *sound* like he was talking?'

I sighed.

'You're weird,' she said.

'Haven't you got some Barbies to annoy?' I asked.

'Can I play with the *hamster* instead? I'll be careful this time.'

Stinky shuddered.

He was probably more scared of my sister than he was of heights.

She sometimes sneaked into my room when I wasn't here and took him out of his

cage to cuddle him and dress him up. He was
becoming too chubby for Barbie clothes, but
the clothes for her My Little Ponies were just
the right size.

Stinky wasn't a huge fan of wearing frilly tutus. Or of having the breath squeezed out of him by seven-year-old girls.

'No, you can't play with him,' I told Lucy. 'Not now. And not ever. Now buzz off, please.'

Which wasn't a very clever thing to say. Even with the 'please' at the end.

Because she *did* buzz off. Straight to Mum and Dad.

Chapter 7

When Mum and Dad came to my room *together* it usually meant I'd done something really bad. But this time they didn't look angry at all. They looked worried.

They sat down next to each other on my bed, and Mum reached forward to give my hand a gentle squeeze.

'Lucy told us you were speaking to your hamster again, Ben.'

I could hardly breathe. Stinky looked petrified.

'Most kids,' my dad added sadly, 'have actual *friends*. But not you. No, you're in your room all the time, building a rocket and talking to your hamster. It's a bit . . .' he was trying to find the right word, '*odd*.'

'Very odd,' my mum said.

'It's very, very odd,' Dad repeated, 'for a nine-year-old boy to be best friends with a rodent. He's only got a brain the size of a pea, Ben. You need to spend more time with *people*.'

I sighed with relief. They *didn't* know about Stinky after all. They just thought he was a regular hamster, and that I was going a bit nutty.

'So we've made a decision,' Mum said.

When both my parents waited for the other to speak, I imagined the worst.

'*Please* don't get rid of Stinky,' I begged them. '*Please* don't give him to another family. *Anything* but that.'

'Don't be daft,' my mum said. 'Of course we won't. What makes you think that? He's a part of the family. We can't give Stinky away, just like we can't give you away, or Lucy.'

I was about to suggest that giving Lucy away might not be such a bad idea after all, but then I changed my mind. It probably wasn't the right time.

'You need to be with other kids more, Ben,' my mum continued. 'So a few moments ago I spoke to Bella next door.'

I gulped. Bella was Edward's mum. She was a colourful, slightly scary lady who ran an umbrella shop – Bella's Umbrellas.

'I think it's crazy,' my mum went on, 'that there's a boy from your class living just next door, and you *never* play together. So you're going round there tomorrow.'

'Oh, Mum!' I said, but she gave me one of

those 'don't argue' looks that she saves for special occasions.

When they left my room, it was raining again. This was actually a *good* thing because the raindrops slapping the window drowned

out the sound of Stinky complaining.

'Your dad spent half an hour looking for his *shoes* yesterday,' Stinky said, looking furious. 'And *I'm* the one who's pea-brained?'

'Sorry about that,' I said. 'But I've got bigger problems – I've got to go to Edward's house tomorrow.'

'But that's actually *good* news,' Stinky said. 'Think about it.'

'Good news? How can a play date with the world's most horrible kid be good news?'

'Well, you'll be *in his house*. You can do some detective work in there. Discover what the pipes in the flying saucer are for. Find out what he's up to.'

'I can't just ask him though, Stinky.'

He sighed. 'Of course I don't want you to ask him. He wouldn't tell you anyway. No – just do some snooping.'

'But how can I, when I'll be with him the whole time? Hey, wait a minute –'

'Oh no,' Stinky said. 'I know what you're thinking, but I'm absolutely *not* coming with you. It's completely out of the question. They have a *cat*.'

'No, they don't. That's *Mrs Gilligan's* cat, Bruiser. She's next door on the other side. The Eggingtons only have a goldfish. You're not scared of goldfish, are you?'

'Actually,' he said, 'goldfish are one of the very few animals that *don't* like to eat hamsters. And I can't believe I'm saying this, but . . . OK, I'll come. If you absolutely promise not to drop me.'

'I promise,' I said.

Chapter 8

We had some of the worst next-door neighbours in the world.

On one side was Mrs Gilligan, who lived

with her cat, and who hadn't smiled (my dad said) for seven years. Her garden was known as The Graveyard. If something went over that fence – a ball or a frisbee – it *never* came back.

Our neighbours on the other side were just as horrible: the Eggingtons.

Bella Eggington was a big woman with red frizzy hair. When she opened the door to me she was wearing a bright green dress, so she looked like a gigantic lime jelly, with a big strawberry on top.

'Come in,' she said. 'Can I take your coat?'

'No, thanks,' I said, stepping nervously into the Eggingtons' house – a huge bungalow – for the first time.

'*Eddie!*' she yelled – so loud it almost burst my eardrums – **'Ben's here!'** Maybe it wasn't only *my* mum who shouted like this. Maybe it was a mum thing. But there was no answer.

'That boy.' She shook her head. 'Always blowing things up.'

Sure enough, I could hear explosions from down the hall. Stinky was twitching nervously in my coat pocket. I must have looked pretty nervous myself, because Mrs Eggington said:

'It's only a computer game he's playing, you know. Follow me.'

We went down the hall towards the noise, past the bathroom and past a door with a 'Top Secret' sign on it.

'That's where they do their experiments,' she explained. 'We keep it locked all the time.'

But the gap at the bottom of the door, I noticed, was just enough for a flexible rodent to squeeze through.

She led me to Edward's room and ushered me in. The noise was deafening.

'Ben's here, Eddie!' she boomed, and then left, trapping me inside as she closed the door.

'If it isn't Beany Boy!' Edward said, not taking his eyes off the computer game on the big screen. 'Baked-Bean Ben!'

He'd come up with those nicknames himself, and most kids in our class thought they were pretty funny. Me, I wasn't such a huge fan.

I stood there, watching him blast aliens for a while. And then he actually turned to me.

'Let's play WrestleSlam,' he said, tossing me a controller. He tutted as I fumbled it and it landed on my toe. (My hamster was right. I *was* always dropping things. My dad says I couldn't catch a *cold*.)

I soon realised why Edward was letting me play: it was a chance for him to beat me up. OK, so it was only a computer game, but he really seemed to be enjoying it. His wrestler was throwing mine around, and jumping on him and thumping him in a fury.

'Take that, you wimp!' Edward gurgled. 'How do you like *that*?'

I didn't. So after a few minutes of being pummelled, I said I needed the toilet and left the room.

In the hall I glanced around. There was no sign of his mum, and there had been no car on the drive, so his dad must be out. This was our chance.

I took Stinky carefully out of my pocket and placed him gently on the carpet in front of the Top Secret room.

He stepped over and pressed his nose up to the door, as if he was trying to sniff out the best way to get inside. Then he crouched so his belly was against the carpet and tried to burrow under the door. At first it looked like he might be stuck there. It was a very tight

squeeze. His bottom wriggled as he strained to fit through the narrow gap.

'Can I help?' I said to his bottom, but with one final effort he managed to squirm underneath the door. And with that he disappeared out of sight.

Chapter 9

I came back from the toilet and stood in the hall, waiting for Stinky and feeling more nervous as time ticked by. We'd agreed on five minutes, but it was already longer than that.

What if there were mousetraps in there, or something else dangerous? What if he didn't come out at all? I stared at the tiny gap between the door and the carpet, silently begging him to appear.

At last I saw him. First his nose and whiskers emerged, and then, after some effort, his

URRGGGH!!!!

URRGGGHHHH!!!!

whole head was poking out.

He eventually managed to squeeze his body through and, just as Stinky was nearly out in the hallway with me, his bottom got wedged. He wriggled desperately.

For a genius, Stinky's timing was terrible. Because at that same moment, Edward's mum came round the corner and spotted him instantly.

'A rat!' she yelped. Stinky was on the carpet, staring back at her, frozen in fear. Bella Eggington's face was by now a kind of purple. 'Squash it!' she screamed at me.

Squish it! Kill it!

The awful noise coming from her mouth got even Edward's attention. He burst out of his room.

'A rat, Eddie!' his mum screeched, pointing at Stinky.

'I'll get it,' he said, marching over. With no time to waste, I blocked his way and rushed over to Stinky myself, grabbing his two front paws to pull him free. There was a faint *pop!* as his bottom unplugged from the door. I scooped him up and covered him with both hands so they couldn't see he was actually a hamster.

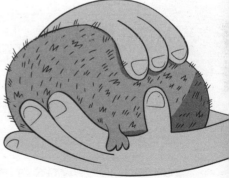

'Choke it!' Mrs Eggington was yelling at me. 'Strangle it! Throttle it!'

'Give that here, Beany Boy,' said Edward Eggington, striding over to me. 'It's in *our* house. So it's *our* property. My father and I can use it for experiments. Give it to me!'

'Never,' I said.

We stared at each other for a few seconds, and then he lunged at me. I dodged him, then rushed out of the house, past a bewildered Mrs Eggington, and ran the very short distance home.

When I put Stinky back into his cage in my room, both of us were panting.

'What a completely awful family,' he wheezed. 'They make *your* family seem quite reasonable. What a horribly rude boy. And what a nasty, rodent-hating woman. And I haven't met Mr Eggington yet, but I *do* know what he's up to.'

'Oh?'

Stinky took a few moments to get his breath back.

'Yes. And it's not nice. Not nice at all. I saw the design for the flying saucer, Ben. Those pipes on the top spray a special mix of chemicals into the air. And that mixture makes it *rain*.'

I frowned.

'Is that even possible? I thought you needed clouds for rain.'

'Those people,' he said, 'made a Snow Machine. If they can do that, they can certainly make it *rain*, don't you think? And didn't you

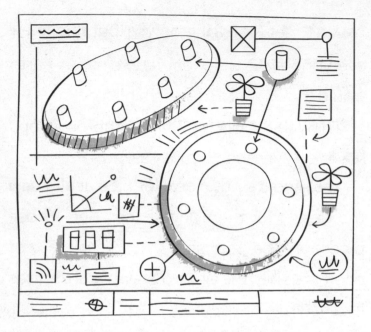

wonder why there was so much of it around here recently?'

'Not really,' I admitted.

'There was a heavy shower last night, for instance,' Stinky said. 'Just after we saw the flying saucer in fact.'

I was completely puzzled. 'But doesn't everyone *hate* wet weather? Why on earth would they want to make it rain?'

'Think about this: how many umbrella shops have you ever seen?' Stinky asked.

'Not many.'

'Don't you think it's strange that Mrs Eggington has one?'

I shrugged. 'Not really. I guess it's because of her name – Bella's Umbrellas. You know – it rhymes. If her name was Sue, she have started a shoe shop. Or a zoo.'

Stinky sighed. He was running out of patience.

'Think about it,' he said, speaking very slowly, like he was explaining something to a very

little kid. '*Umbrellas*. The flying saucer makes it rain and rain, so Mrs Eggington sells lots and lots of umbrellas. And so the Eggingtons become very rich.'

'Oh!' I said. It *was* a pretty clever plan. 'The question is – how can we stop them?'

'While I was in the Top Secret room,' Stinky explained, 'I nibbled through some of the flying saucer's wires. Hopefully they won't realise what I've done until it's too late – until the day of the competition, that is.'

'But what if they notice and fix it?'

He shrugged. 'Then,' he said, 'we're all going to get very wet indeed.'

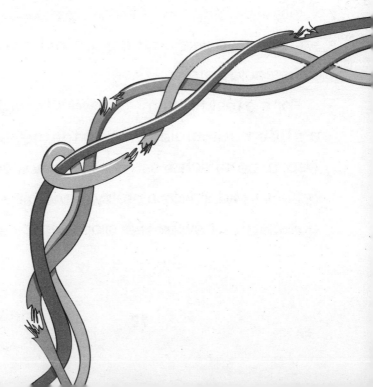

Chapter 10

One week before the big competition, my dad was on his hands and knees in the garden, making sure the rocket was pointing straight up, and I was standing next to him. Stinky's cage was on the grass in the corner, so he could watch too.

For the test flight, my dad would be lighting the fuse, but it would be my turn on the big day. Also, to be safe, the astronaut today was one of Lucy's My Little Ponies. It was the same size and weight as a hamster, although of course a plastic toy wouldn't be able to perform any of the amazing tricks that Stinky would be attempting.

'Is it *two* teaspoons of rocket fuel, Ben?' my dad asked. He thought I was some kind of rocket scientist now. I nodded, and he carefully added the fuel (Stinky's special recipe) to the section at the bottom of the rocket.

It was then that I heard a small voice.

I spun around and saw next door's cat, Bruiser, hissing at Stinky and rattling his cage. I sprinted over, waving my arms crazily and shooing the cat away. Bruiser sprang off and slunk through the hole in the fence, back to Mrs Gilligan's garden.

My dad, meanwhile, was baffled.

'Did you say something?' he asked.

'I said, "Shoo!"'

'*Before* that. I distinctly heard someone say, "Help!"'

I shrugged.

Dad paused and frowned at me. And then he went inside to fetch the matches.

My hamster was still trembling.

'It's only a cat, Stinky,' I whispered. 'Calm down a bit.'

'*Calm down?*' he panted. '*Calm down?* Imagine there's a vicious animal ten times *your* size that wants to eat *you*, and now imagine it's so close to you that you can smell its disgusting fishy breath. *Then you try calming down!'*

'Shh,' I said, because my dad was bounding back with the box of matches.

'Do a countdown,' Dad said excitedly. 'Like they do for the space shuttles.'

Stinky glared at me while I took up my position in the corner of the garden.

'**10, 9, 8, 7,**' I said, as Dad lit the fuse and stood back beside me –

'**6, 5, 4, 3, 2, 1 . . .**' My voice went all wobbly with excitement. **'Blast off!'**

Then . . .

Nothing.

We all stared at the rocket, which was doing absolutely nothing.

I sighed. Nothing ever went to plan.

And then ...

Whoosh!

Chapter 11

My dad, my hamster and I all tilted our heads back to see the rocket whizzing straight up, leaving a trail of smoke behind it.

'Wow,' I said.

'Blimey,' said Dad. 'Look how high it's going! It'll come back down with snow on it!'

I looked over at Stinky and I think I saw him smile, although it *is* really hard to tell with hamsters.

The rocket was so high now that it looked tiny – then it slowed and turned around so it was suddenly dropping back towards us. I held my breath. Would the parachute pop open? Yes! And now the rocket was floating slowly back to Earth.

But not back to *us*.

The breeze was enough to blow the rocket off course, and we watched helplessly as it drifted away from us, and over towards Mrs Gilligan's garden. The parachute got lower and lower until it snagged in the outer branches of her big oak tree. It was only just over her side of the fence, but even with a ladder, we wouldn't be able to reach it.

'Oh,' my dad said, as we stared at the rocket hanging there. 'Oh dear.'

I couldn't speak.

It had all been going so well, but now it might be over.

Mrs Gilligan's garden – The Graveyard – was full of balls and frisbees and any other toys that had had the misfortune to land there.

'OK,' my dad said. 'Stay calm. I know what you're thinking, but let's get Stinky inside, and – very politely – let's go and ask for it back.'

Mrs Gilligan was an old lady with long grey hair, a wart on her nose and a broomstick. OK, I made up the bit about the broomstick, but all the kids in the street thought she might have been a witch. She *did* have a black cat of course.

My dad knocked on her door. I was behind him, nervous, and even Dad looked a bit uneasy. The door creaked open and there was Mrs Gilligan in a long black dress. Bruiser was at her feet, not so much *purring* as *snarling*. The cat and the owner were just as bad-tempered as each other.

'Oh,' she said. 'It's you. Your ball's in my garden again, I suppose. Well, you know the rules.'

'Not *ball* exactly, no,' my dad explained. 'It's actually a science project.'

'A science project?'

'A rocket, to be exact.'

'A *rocket*?'

'In your tree.'

'I *wondered* what that dreadful noise was just now. What on *earth* are you thinking of, launching missiles in a quiet, calm street like this? Of course, when I say "quiet" and "calm",' she added sourly, 'I'm most certainly *not* including *your* family. The hideous racket that girl makes with her tap-dancing, for instance, is neither quiet nor calm. Nor is that foghorn voice of your wife, calling everyone to tea. It's noise pollution, is what it is. So no, you will *not* get your rocket back. And if you so much as *think* about sneaking into my garden to fetch it, I'll call the police. Good day.'

And, with that, she slammed the door in our faces.

Chapter 12

The worst thing was looking out of the window and seeing the rocket just dangling there in the outer branches of Mrs Gilligan's big oak tree. It was so close, but tantalisingly out of reach.

Dad and I had given up hope of ever getting it back.

My hamster, though, had a plan.

I'd really thought he'd be relieved that the rocket was gone. After all, that meant he didn't have to fly any more. But he actually seemed disappointed, like he secretly *wanted* to be an astronaut now.

I told my dad the plan. He looked at me, impressed, and promised to help too. He wanted the rocket back as much as I did, because he was in big trouble with my mum and Lucy – not really for losing the *rocket*, but because of the My Little Pony that was inside it.

It took us an hour to get everything ready, and then Dad and I stood in the garden. I put Stinky's cage on the windowsill this time. He could still see from there, but Bruiser couldn't get at him.

We'd taken an old kite from the shed and superglued some fridge magnets to the middle of it. Now all we needed was for the wind to change direction.

I picked a few blades of grass and threw them in the air to check what the wind was doing, like Stinky had taught me.

Yes! Finally it was blowing towards Mrs Gilligan's house, so we sprang into action. Dad threw the kite high into the air, and I held tight on to the strings.

The kite was tricky to control at first, but I soon got the hang of it. When it was at the right height, I edged closer and closer to the tree, careful not to get the kite tangled too.

'Whooaa!' my dad said, waving his arms as the kite brushed against the branches right near to the rocket. 'A bit to the left! Now a bit to the right! That's it!'

I could hear the magnet clink against the rocket and stick to it immediately. But then the kite was suddenly too heavy of course. I tugged sharply on the strings, like I'd caught a really big fish and was desperately trying to reel it in.

The kite and rocket plummeted, clipped the top of the fence – and fell into *our* garden.

'Woo-hoo! shouted my dad, and he tore around the garden with his arms up like he'd scored the winner in the Cup Final. I was leaping about too, yelling with delight.

I looked at Stinky and I think I saw him grinning inside his cage. Though, as I say, it *is* very hard to tell with hamsters.

Chapter 13

It was the morning of the science fair.

'I'm hungry,' Stinky whispered. For someone who was much smaller than a pencil case, he had a really big appetite, and he always seemed to eat more when he was nervous.

I came back from the kitchen with a handful of lettuce and pushed it through the bars of his cage. He started nibbling straight away.

'Very funny, by the way,' he mumbled.

'What's very funny?'

'This lettuce.'

I frowned at him. Maybe he was so scared about being an astronaut that he'd lost his mind. No one had ever called lettuce *funny* before. *Boring*, yes. *Green*, yes. *Funny*, never.

'What's so funny about it?'

'The name, obviously,' he said. 'This type of lettuce is called "rocket". I thought it was your clever little joke.' Then he saw my blank expression. 'I should have known better of course,' he added.

I fished something out of my pocket.

'I made you this,' I told him.

He glanced up from his lettuce. 'It looks,' he said, 'very much like half a table-tennis ball.'

'It's a crash helmet,' I told him. 'And I've got a spare one exactly like it.'

He sighed as I put it on to his head. 'Do you really suppose,' he started, 'that if something goes wrong and I plummet to Earth at sixty-seven kilometres an hour in a metal cylinder – do you really think that half a ping-pong ball will protect me?'

'Maybe,' I said.

'My life,' he said, shaking his head, 'is in the hands of a nincompoop.'

When I took off his crash helmet, he paced up and down in his cage.

'You seem nervous, Stinky.'

'That's because I *am* nervous.'

'Me too.'

'You? Are *you* going to be hurtling into the sky in a baked-bean tin, with half a ping-pong ball on your head? *I thought not.* So what do *you* have to be nervous about? You humans – always worrying when there's nothing to worry about.'

'I'm worried about *you*, Stinky. I don't want you to do it any more. Honest. I was selfish to ask you in the first place. I've realised that winning isn't nearly as important as having a friend. Even a grumpy one. Let's just fly the rocket without an astronaut – there's a word for that, isn't there?'

'The word is *unmanned*. An "unmanned" flight. Or "unhamstered" in this case. But, no, Ben, you don't understand. I can't back out now. I actually *want* to do it. In fact I *need* to do it.'

'If it's about the carrots, I'll get you some anyway –'

'It's not about that,' he said. 'And neither is it really about beating Edward Eggington and his rodent-hating family. Though obviously that would be rather nice. No. It's about *me*. I've decided that the best way of overcoming my fear is to confront it.'

'What do you mean?'

'I'm afraid of heights,' he said. 'Which isn't nice if you spend your whole life on a desk. Or being carried around by a boy who's constantly dropping things. So today I'm going to go higher than any rodent has ever gone before. And after that I won't be frightened any more.'

He looked pretty scared now though. He went for a very long run on his wheel.

Chapter 14

The science fair was crowded, with lots of domes scattered around a big field: huge round tents like upside-down cereal bowls, one for each of the planets, plus another two for the Sun and the Moon.

There were loads of stalls too: food stalls, stalls selling science kits, and one big umbrella stall.

'I don't fancy Bella's chances of selling too many umbrellas today,' my dad said, looking up. 'Not a dark cloud in the sky. Now, where's the competition tent?'

It took us ages to find it. By the time we got there, most of the other kids had already set up. Each kid had been given a stand (actually a small table) with their name on it. My dad had gone off to find a toilet, and I went to look for my stand. It was just my luck that it was next to Edward Eggington's.

'Hello, Beany Boy,' he said with a smirk, as I put my rocket proudly on my stand, and the pot of rocket fuel next to it 'This is a *science* competition. The recycling bin's over *there*.'

'Ha ha,' I said. 'Funny joke. Did your dad help you to think of that one?'

I put my backpack very carefully on the floor under the table.

Inside it was a big roll of paper and an old

lunchbox with holes punched into it. Inside *that*, of course, was my hamster.

I pulled the roll of paper – the *cylinder* of paper – out of the bag, unrolled it and sticky-taped it to my table. For the competition, each kid needed something explaining what we'd made. I'd done mine in colourful felt-tip, in the shape of a rocket.

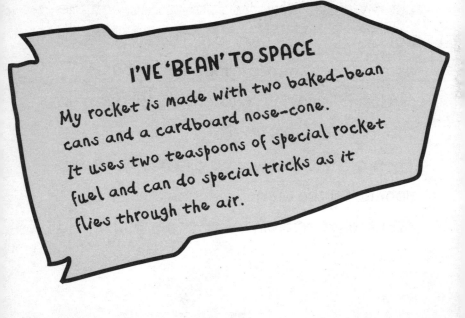

I'VE 'BEAN' TO SPACE

My rocket is made with two baked-bean cans and a cardboard nose-cone. It uses two teaspoons of special rocket fuel and can do special tricks as it flies through the air.

Edward Eggington's information, however, was on a big computer screen behind him, with 3D animation of his flying saucer:

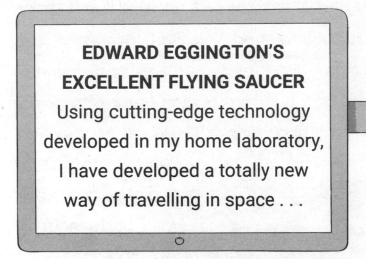

EDWARD EGGINGTON'S EXCELLENT FLYING SAUCER
Using cutting-edge technology developed in my home laboratory, I have developed a totally new way of travelling in space . . .

I could read the whole thing from my stand. There were lots of words I didn't understand, although there was no mention at all of pipes or chemicals. Or rain.

I could see a few of the other entries.

An older boy had made a remote-control moon buggy. A girl had made a brilliant model of the solar system where all the planets revolved around the Sun. Someone had made a little telescope, and someone else had built a huge model of Saturn, complete with cardboard rings. There was another Sun, which lit up like a big orange beach ball, and a model of a space station made out of Lego.

Stinky had told me he was going to write a word in the sky with the rocket – 'hello' in joined-up writing. That would be fantastic – and it would have to be, to have any chance of winning.

'Winning's not everything, son,' said my dad, who must have been thinking the same thing. 'Let's have a look around the universe, shall we?'

'I think I'll just wait here,' I said, because I didn't want to leave Stinky alone, but Dad insisted. 'We'll only be a few minutes. A walk around will do us good.'

I nodded and reluctantly followed him around the field. Inside each of the planet domes was a TV screen with a little movie, pictures and a real science person with lots of interesting information.

We popped in to Jupiter and learned that it was by far the biggest planet – so big that you could fit all the other seven planets into it. Plus there's a storm on Jupiter which is three times bigger than Earth and which has been going on pretty much *forever*.

'Good grief,' Dad said to the lady who had all the information. 'You'd need a pretty good umbrella on Jupiter.' He nudged me and grinned. 'Bella Eggington might have more luck there, eh, son?'

'It's actually a *gas* planet,' the lady said, 'and is minus 200 degrees on the outside. So I think you'd need a bit more than an umbrella.'

After Jupiter, we walked past the red tent of Mars (which was too busy), and into Earth. I didn't think it would be too exciting, seeing as we spend all our time here anyway, but I was wrong. The man in there told us that – at this very moment – this planet was spinning around at more than 1,000 kilometres an hour: much faster than an aeroplane.

'Crikey,' said Dad. 'I feel dizzy just *thinking* about it. I think I need to sit down. So, how come we don't all fall off?'

I answered even before the man could.

'It's called "gravity", Dad.'

Dad looked impressed. The man too.

Stinky had taught me about gravity. He'd taught me a lot, my hamster.

I wondered how he was feeling, and asked Dad if – instead of visiting Venus – I could go back to prepare for the launch.

He nodded, said he'd see me in a few minutes, went to Venus by himself, and I went back to the tent. But when I got back to my stand and looked into my backpack, the lunchbox was open!

I gasped. Stinky was gone.

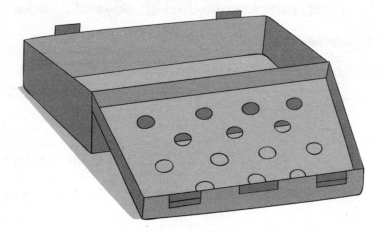

Chapter 15

I looked around, my heart thumping. There was no sign of him. Had someone stolen him?

Had he got so scared he'd run away?

A busy science fair was no place for a loose hamster, not even a genius one. There were so many feet around. I sank desperately to my hands and knees to look for him.

'Psst! Ben! Over here!'

My whole body tingled with relief when I spotted Stinky hiding behind a table leg.

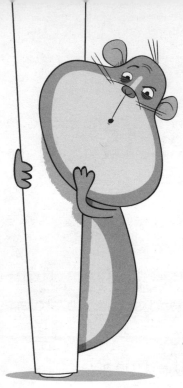

I could have kissed him. I didn't of course. His fur would've been far too tickly, for one thing. Instead I reached out, scooped him up and put him gently back into his box, and put that in the backpack. Then I looked around. Although the tent was busy, most people were crowded around Edward Eggington's stand, inspecting the flying saucer. Luckily no one was paying attention to me or my rocket.

Still on the ground, I put my head into

the backpack. This way, if anyone *did* look over here, they'd think I was searching for something inside.

'You OK?' I whispered.

'I think so,' he panted.

'What were you doing outside your box? You could've been squished.'

'I *know*. but I couldn't stay there.'

'Why not?'

'I suspected sabotage.'

'What? What does that even *mean*?'

'It means that I thought someone was trying to wreck our rocket. And that someone,' he announced, 'was none other than Edward Eggington. I heard him walking over to our stand when no one was around.'

'You were in the lunchbox. How did you know it was him?'

'Edward Eggington,' Stinky explained, 'has squeaky shoes. If there's one thing that we rodents know about, it's things that squeak. Plus, my ears may be tiny, but they're extremely sensitive. Your huge, flappy ears, on the other hand –'

'Get to the point,' I interrupted. 'What was Eggington doing?'

'That's what I didn't know. Hence me

nudging open the box and wriggling out of the bag. I knew I had to investigate.'

'And?'

'He was already walking back to his stand by the time I got out. I'm not sure if he did anything. It's possible he was just having a look, but I *would* like to inspect the rocket closely, to make sure.'

I took the rocket from the table and put it carefully into the bag, so no one would see Stinky checking it out. He scurried about in there for a while.

'It *looks* exactly the same,' he reported.

'I don't think you should fly, Stinky. Just in case he *has* done something to the rocket. Sabo-*whatsit*.'

'Sabo*tage*,' he said. 'Look – do you think I've come all this way to sit in a lunchbox?'

And with that he climbed into the astronaut compartment, saying:

Chapter 16

The launch area was this huge roped-off circle, with lots of people around it looking in. Miss Miles was there, smiling encouragingly. I stood next to Dad, just inside the rope, clutching the rocket with Stinky inside. We were ready.

The Eggingtons were first to go, and they looked really confident, waving to the crowd as if they were celebrities. Two umbrellas were lying on the ground beside them. An official in a bright yellow jacket handed Edward a microphone so he could address the crowd.

'I, Edward Eggington, last year's winner, proudly introduce my incredible flying saucer. Stand back and prepare to be amazed.'

With that, he pressed a button on the controller, and the flying saucer slowly rose from the ground. It climbed and climbed until it was hovering high above us all. I had to admit, it did look impressive.

It seemed as if the Eggingtons had fixed Stinky's attempt at sabotage. The spectators were clapping and ooh-ing and aah-ing, but not me – I knew that we were all about to get soaked, and there was nothing I could do to stop it.

But when Edward Eggington pressed another button, it didn't rain. Instead the flying saucer started wobbling around crazily like a spinning plate.

Edward was now trying desperately to stop the experiment. He was jabbing at buttons on his controller, but it was no good. Then his dad snatched the control from him and tried the same, but all that happened was that the flying saucer flipped around and around like a tossed coin. I was getting dizzy just watching it. And then . . .

BANG!

The whole thing exploded.

Tiny bits of the flying saucer rained down onto the Eggingtons like silver confetti. Some of the crowd laughed, and others clapped like they were watching a firework display.

The Eggingtons weren't laughing or clapping though. Not at all. Edward glared at his dad, who was shaking his head in disbelief and muttering. Then they both stomped off, arguing.

I whispered to Stinky to tell him what had happened, but we had no time to celebrate, because it was our turn next.

Someone announced my name and we were ushered into the middle of the circle. Dad helped make sure the rocket was pointing straight up, then he took a few steps back. I knelt by the rocket, trembling with nerves and excitement.

'Good luck, Stinky,' I whispered. 'You know, it's not too late if you want to change your mind . . .'

'Get on with it,' he snapped.

The man in the bright yellow jacket handed me the microphone and asked me to introduce myself and my rocket to the crowd.

When I saw how many people were staring at me, I went all wobbly, and I could hardly hold the microphone, let alone speak.

'Hello,' I mumbled. 'I'm Ben. Ben Jinks. And this is my rocket. It's made out of bean cans.' There was a bit of uncomfortable laughter. 'And I hope it will write a word in the sky.' More laughter.

I couldn't think of anything more to say, so I lit the fuse and stood back beside my dad, a safe distance away. I was far too nervous to do a countdown. I could only imagine how

my hamster was feeling, sitting there in a can,

about to be shot up into the sky.

It was hard to breathe.

And then . . .

Whooooossssshhhhh!

Up, up, up zoomed the rocket, leaving a thin white trail of smoke. The crowd, suddenly, was clapping and whooping.

But something didn't seem right. It only took me a second to realise what it was: the rocket was going too fast, much faster than the test flight in our garden. This time it was a blur, shooting higher and higher, and it wasn't slowing down. Suddenly I knew what Edward Eggington had done to

118

sabotage it. The rocket had looked the same because it *was* the same, but he'd added more fuel. Much more.

Bravely, Stinky was trying to write in the sky, but the rocket was too fast to control and the writing was all wobbly. The trail of smoke made a clumsy 'h' as he twisted around, and then an 'e', and after that he soared up for a loopy 'l', but then . . .

Either he lost control, and the second 'l' and the 'o' merged together – or else he was sending me a message. Because the word left in the sky wasn't '*hello*' but '*help*'.

Then the rocket zoomed straight up like a giant exclamation mark, rushing further and further away until it was a tiny dot.

And then it was so far away that even the dot disappeared. Me and Dad and the entire crowd were left looking at absolutely nothing.

There was a huge round of applause and quite a few cheers, but I felt like crying.

'Crikey,' my dad muttered.

I was completely speechless, still staring at the empty sky.

Was my hamster lost in space?

My brain took a few seconds to get going again.

Stinky had told me there was *no way* that a little rocket like ours could go into space. Not even if it was *full* of rocket fuel.

And as Stinky had also taught me, what goes up must come down. That was *gravity*. But *where* would he come down? That was the question.

OK. Think, think . . .

One more thing that I'd learned from my hamster was how to check the direction of the wind. I bent down, tore up some grass and threw it into the air. The wind was blowing towards the Moon. Not the actual Moon, of course. The Moon *tent*.

So I sprinted off, ducked under the rope and squirmed through the crowd. Then I spotted the rocket again. At first it was a speck, but it got bigger as it dropped back to Earth.

But would the parachute work if the rocket was falling from really, really high up?

I stopped running and just stood and stared into the sky, hoping.

The parachute opened. I sighed, and then started running again. It's not easy to run when you're looking straight up. I bumped into lots of people.

The rocket was falling gently towards the top of the Moon tent now. I held my breath as it hit the top of the tent and bounced not far from me.

But, as it bounced, the parachute collapsed, and now the rocket wasn't falling *gently* any

Moon

more – it was suddenly hurtling towards the hard ground. I sidestepped two people, leaped and flung myself at it full stretch, like a goalkeeper, and grabbed it with both hands just above the ground.

I lay there for a few moments. Then I pulled the rocket towards my face, so only Stinky could hear me.

'You OK?' I panted. 'Are you alive?'

There was silence for what seemed like a very long time.

'Alive?' he said eventually. 'I've never *been* more alive. Let's do it again!'

Chapter 17

'Have you noticed,' my mum said at the dinner table the next weekend, 'how it hasn't been raining nearly so much this last week? Hardly at all in fact. More chips, Ben?'

I nodded. It was burgers and chips for tea, my all-time favourite.

'Would you like some more red sauce, Ben?' Lucy asked me.

'Yes, please.'

Lucy had been unusually nice to me since I'd bought her a new pair of tap shoes. I'd

bought some carrots for Stinky too, and given the rest of the prize money to Mum and Dad. They were so proud of me, I could spend as much time as I liked in my bedroom.

Tonight, as usual, I went up straight after my tea.

Stinky had been nibbling on a juicy carrot and looked very happy.

'Next,' he announced, 'I want to try bungee jumping.'

'Hamsters,' I whispered, 'don't bungee jump.'

'Just get me a super-strong elastic band,' he said, 'and I'll show you how.'

'No way,' I told him. 'It's too dangerous.'

'Dangerous? *Dangerous?* You're not talking to just *any* hamster, you know. You're talking to the first hamster to have landed on the Moon.'

'Not the real Moon,' I pointed out. 'And not "landed" either. More "bounced off".'

He squinted at me, and eventually smiled.

'You're quite funny sometimes,' he said. 'For a human.'

I smiled back. He was pretty amazing sometimes.

For a hamster.

THE END

Have you read the other
Stinky and Jinks adventures?

A STINKY AND JINKS ADVENTURE

MY HAMSTER IS A
GENIUS

ILLUSTRATED BY THE BOY FITZ HAMMOND

DAVE LOWE

Piccadilly
PRESS

PICCADILLY
PRESS

A STINKY and JINKS ADVENTURE

MY HAMSTER'S GOT
TALENT

DAVE LOWE

ILLUSTRATED BY
THE BOY FITZ HAMMOND

Piccadilly
PRESS

Dave Lowe grew up in Dudley in the West Midlands, and now lives in Brisbane, Australia, with his wife and two daughters. He spends his days writing books, drinking lots of tea, and treading on Lego that his daughters have left lying around. Dave's Stinky and Jinks books follow the adventures of a nine-year-old boy called Ben, and Stinky, Ben's genius pet hamster. (When Dave was younger, he had a pet hamster too. Unlike Stinky, however, Dave's hamster didn't often help him with his homework.) Find Dave online at @daveloweauthor or www.davelowebooks.com

Born in York in the late 1970s, **The Boy Fitz Hammond** now lives in Edinburgh with his wife and their two sons. A freelance illustrator for well over a decade, he loves to draw in a variety of styles, allowing him to work on a range of projects across all media. Find him online at www.nbillustration.co.uk/the-boy-fitz-hammond or on Twitter @tbfhDotCom

Piccadilly

P R E S S

Thank you for choosing a Piccadilly Press book.

If you would like to know more about our authors, our books or if you'd just like to know what we're up to, you can find us online.

www.piccadillypress.co.uk

You can also find us on:

We hope to see you soon!